cancer
can't STOP us

MEGHAN MURRAY
AUTHOR

PREXIE BELAND
ILLUSTRATOR

Cancer Can't Stop Us Written by Meghan Murray

Illustrated by Prexie Beland.

Dedication:

To the families whose lives have been touched by cancer, especially those who have young girls and boys at home, I hope this book can be a resource for you that provides a source of comfort, hope, or inspiration.

To the countless doctors, nurses, and healthcare professionals whose unwavering dedication and compassion brings hope and healing to patients and their families, thank you.

To my step-dad, Kent, whose courage, strength, and resilience continues to inspire us all day in and day out. I love you.

Once upon a time, there was a family whose home was filled with adventure, love, light, and laughter.

But one day, their home was flipped
upside down when the doctor said that
Maggie's Daddy was sick with a disease named
cancer.

Maggie didn't know what cancer meant, so the doctor explained it in a way that made the most sense.

"Cancer is when our body cells start acting strange, making us feel different and causing a change. This can happen to anyone, big or small, but it can't stop us from standing tall."

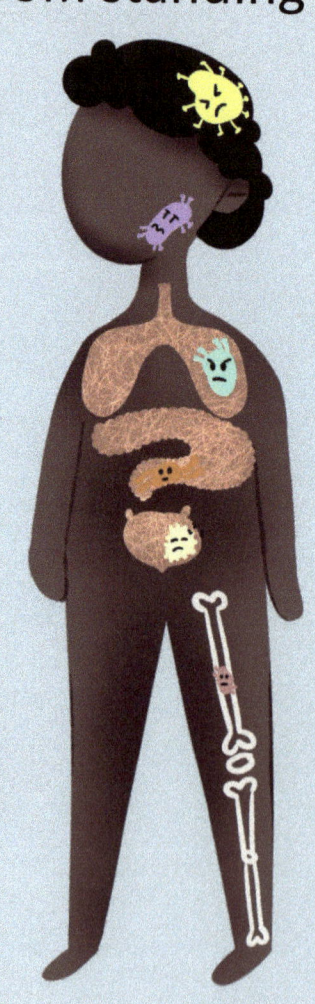

In Daddy's case, the cancer grew in his bladder, and it made him weak, sad, and tired.

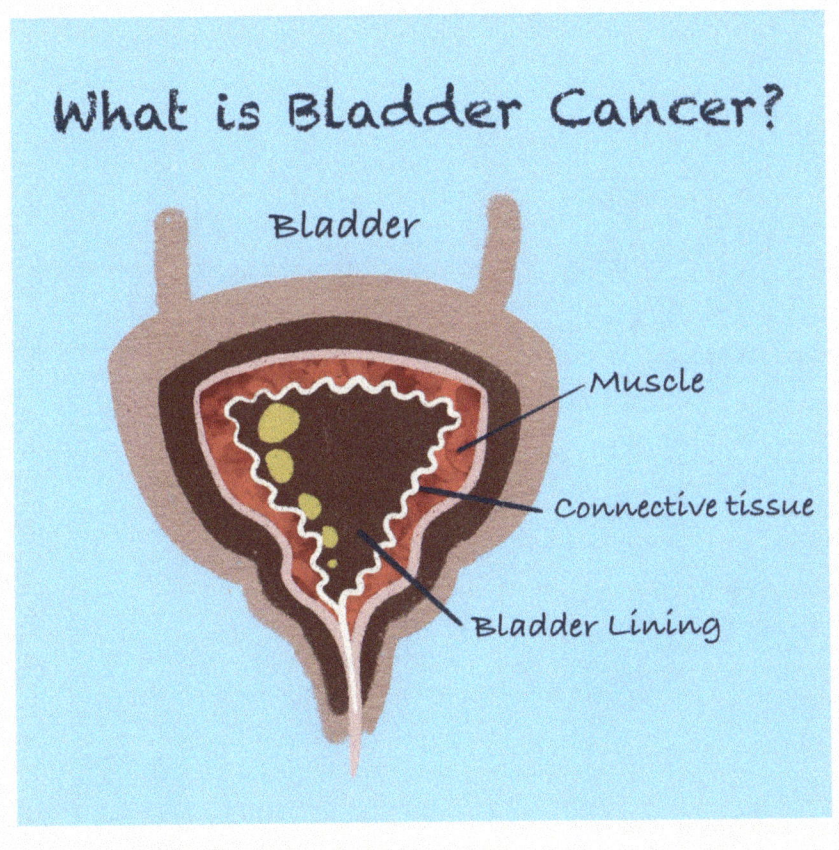

What is Bladder Cancer?

Bladder

Muscle

Connective tissue

Bladder Lining

The doctors said that to make the cancer go away, hospital stays, surgeries, and lots of medicine would be required.

At first, Maggie felt sad, mad, and scared. She didn't want to share her feelings; she didn't want to make her parents feel bad.

But Mommy assured her that her feelings were valid. "It's okay to have big feelings and show that you care," she added.

Some days were filled with laughter and fun.

Especially when they got to play games in the backyard, under the sun.

But other days, her daddy felt too weak
and tired to play,

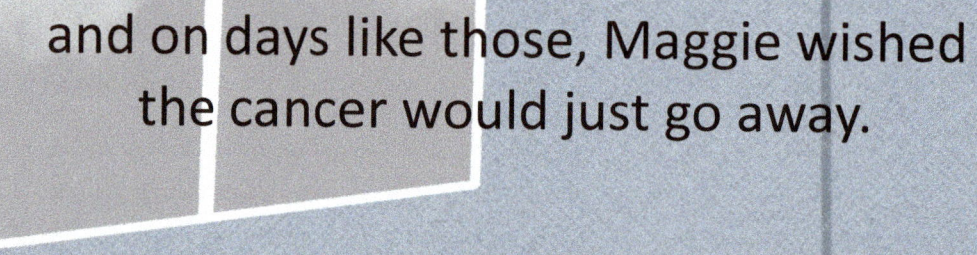

and on days like those, Maggie wished
the cancer would just go away.

12

As the days turned to weeks,
and weeks became months,

Maggie and her family felt love and support from all fronts.

From school friends' hugs, to teammates' cheers,

the neighbours bringing meals, or family members just being there.

One day, the doctor called with news to share:

"the cancer has left," she said. It is all clear.

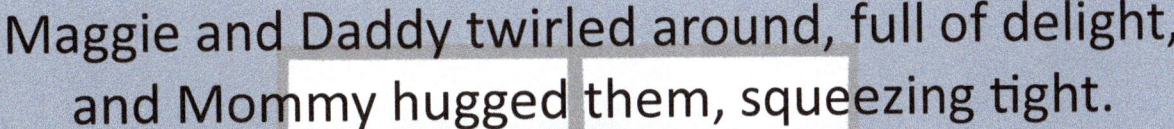

Maggie and Daddy twirled around, full of delight,
and Mommy hugged them, squeezing tight.

Their home echoed with laughter
and cheer, as together they overcame
what they once feared.

Now every day brought joy and glee as they embraced each moment, happy and free.

With daddy healthy and strong once more,
their family bond was even stronger
than before.

Please remember, dear reader, when the skies seem grey, that love and courage can guide you, lighting the way.

With each challenge faced, you'll find the light, just like Maggie's family, who once again are shining bright.

The End!

The Canadian Cancer Society works tirelessly to save and improve lives. We raise funds to fuel the brightest minds in cancer research. We provide a compassionate support system for all those affected by cancer, across Canada and for all types of cancer. Together with patients, supporters, donors and volunteers, we work to create a healthier future for everyone. Because to take on cancer, it takes all of us. It takes a society.

About the Author

Meghan Murray, born and raised in the small, riverside town of Brockville, ON, comes from a big, blended family, and is a business owner, full-time wedding photographer, and the author of "Cancer Can't Stop Us", a book that is a retelling of her and her family's story.

In 2014, nearly a decade ago at the time of publishing, Meghan's step-dad Kent was diagnosed with bladder cancer. As a 10-year-old girl, there weren't many resources that could help her to understand or cope with this massive life event. Her goal is that this book can be that resource - and provide a source of comfort, hope, or inspiration to girls and boys who are going through similar situations as she did all those years ago.